EXPLORING TOUGH ISSUES

Why do people Smoke?

Jillian Powell

RAINTREE
STECK-VAUGHN
PUBLISHERS

RSVP ®

A Harcourt Company

Austin   New York
www.steck-vaughn.com

Published by Raintree Steck-Vaughn Publishers, an imprint of Steck-Vaughn Company

Library of Congress Cataloging-in-Publication Data
Powell, Jillian.
Why do people smoke / Jillian Powell.
    p.   cm.—(Exploring tough issues)
    Includes bibliographical references and index.
    ISBN 0-7398-3234-4
    1. Smoking—Juvenile literature.
    [1. Smoking.]
    I. Title. II. Series.

Printed in Italy. Bound in the United States.
1 2 3 4 5 6 7 8 9 0 05 04 03 02 01

Picture acknowledgments
The publisher would like to thank the following for their kind permission to use their pictures: British Museum 4 (below); Mark Douet *cover*; Eye Ubiquitous (Bennett Dean) 6, (John Dakers) 8, (David Cumming) 30 (above), (K. Wilton) 33, (Gary Trotter) 35, (Paul Seheult) 42 (below); Sally Greenhill 42 (above); HWPL (Angela Hampton) contents page (below), 4 (above), 7, 9, (Zak Waters) 11 (below),12, (APM Studios) 13, (Angus Blackburn) 19, 22, 23, 27, (Rupert Horrox) 29, (Angela Hampton) 31, 39, 40 (both), 44; Impact (Simon Shepheard) 21, (Andy Johnstone) 28, Caroline Penn 32 (above), (Ben Edwards) 38; James Davis Travel Photography 17 (below); Mary Evans Picture Library 5; National Film Archive 10; Panos Pictures (Giacomo Pirozzi) contents page (above), 11 (above); Quadrant Picture Library 36; Science Photo Library (Art Siegel/Custom Medical Stock Photo 16, (Damien Lovegrove) 17 (above), (Colin Cuthbert) 25, (James Stevenson) 26 (below), (Neil Bromhall) 32 (below); Skjold 24; South American Pictures (Tony Morrison) 14, (Rolando Pujol) 34; Roger Vlitos 15, 20, 26 (above), 30 (below), 37, 41; White-Thomson Publishing Ltd *title page*, 18, 43, 45.

IMPORTANT NOTE: Models have been used for all the photos in this book.

Contents

1. How smoking became popular

How was smoking discovered?

Did you know that tobacco was used thousands of years ago? The leaves of the tobacco plant were being chewed or smoked long before people understood what tobacco contained or what it did to their health.

People cultivated tobacco plants in the Americas as early as 6000 B.C. Native Americans smoked peace pipes in religious ceremonies and used tobacco to dress wounds. Chewing tobacco was believed to cure toothaches. The Maya people of Central America smoked tobacco from around A.D. 500. In 1492, Native Americans gave dried tobacco leaves to the explorer Christopher Columbus as a gift. Soon after, tobacco was being grown all over Europe. Some doctors believed that tobacco could cure anything from bad breath to cancer.

▲ *Native Americans believed that smoking tobacco could cure everything from toothaches to earaches. Sometimes, they mixed tobacco leaves with other plants to change the flavor.*

▶ *Native American pipes were often works of art. Each man kept his own special pipe, although it was often passed around a group to be smoked.*

This man is sniffing powdered tobacco, called snuff. In the 18th century, snuff took over in Europe as the fashionable way to use tobacco.

By the 1600s, tobacco had become so popular in Europe that it was often used as money. During the 1700s, smoking fell out of fashion when using tobacco in the form of snuff became popular. But in the 1800s, the first cigarette factories opened, and cigarettes were produced in large numbers.

The first health warnings came after nicotine—the drug in tobacco—was discovered in 1826. In the United States, Samuel Green stated that tobacco was a poison that could kill people.

Yet cigarettes were handed out to soldiers during World War I (1914–18). Also, many women began to smoke, especially as more of them went to work outside the home. By the 1920s and 1930s, smoking had become fashionable. But during the 1950s, medical reports began to appear linking smoking with lung cancer.

FACT:
People did not really understand that smoking could cause deadly diseases until quite recently. In the 1950s, the first major studies in the United States and Great Britain linked smoking with lung cancer.

Tobacco

Cigarettes, cigars, and pipes all contain tobacco, made from the leaves of the tobacco plant. To make cigarettes, the leaves are dried, shredded, and mixed with chemicals to keep them moist, then rolled in paper. As the tobacco burns, the smoke is breathed into the body.

◀ *This boy in China is holding tobacco leaves that have been dried in the sun.*

The Native American peoples found that chewing or smoking tobacco could calm their nerves and make them feel relaxed. This effect comes from the drug nicotine, which is in the tobacco leaves. When people smoke or chew tobacco, nicotine gets into their bloodstream. The drug quickly reaches the smokers' brains and begins to make them feel good.

"Nicotiana tabacum — the tobacco plant, the most dangerous plant on the planet, currently killing around 4 million people annually." *GASP Smoke-free Solutions*

case study · case study · case study ·

Marion has been a smoker nearly all her life. She cannot imagine getting through the day without her cigarettes. She keeps them by her bed so she can light up when she wakes in the morning. Most days, she smokes about two packs.

Marion knows that her cough is caused by smoking, and last year she had to stay in the hospital because of heart trouble. The doctors told her she was damaging her health and should give up cigarettes.

Marion knows her health is bad, but she is not willing to give up the things she enjoys most. Her work on the telephone switchboard is really boring, and she has lived on her own since getting a divorce. She feels she needs cigarettes just to get through the day. Marion tells her doctor she will try to quit smoking, but secretly she feels you have to die from something, and it might as well be from something you enjoy.

▼ *Marion really enjoys her cigarettes and is not willing to give them up.*

7

Smoking—a global habit

Today, about a third of all adults worldwide—1.1 billion people—are smokers. In the United States, approximately 50 million people are smokers. In the developed world, the number of smokers has been falling because more is known about the health risks, and there are now more anti-smoking laws. But in countries such as China, Russia, and Poland, the number of smokers is increasing, especially among young people. China is now the world's largest producer and consumer of tobacco. The number of cigarettes smoked per person in the population more than doubled between 1965 and 1990. Eastern Europe is also a growing market. Russia is now the third largest market for tobacco consumption, after China and the United States.

"In industrialized countries, cigarette consumption fell 10% from 1970 to 1994 but in developing nations it rose 67%."
World Health Organization

As smoking begins in a country, it follows this pattern:
♦ men take it up first
♦ the number of men smoking rises rapidly, then falls
♦ boys begin to smoke, following the same pattern as men
♦ women start smoking
♦ finally, girls take up the habit.

▶ *Young women in Tokyo, Japan. In Japan, the number of young women smokers rose by more than 5 percent between 1970 and 1990.*

Worldwide, poor and unemployed people are most likely to become regular smokers. Tobacco costs and use add to the problems of poverty and disease for people in the developing world. Smokers who are poor may choose between buying cigarettes and food. In Bangladesh, if a man smokes just five cigarettes a day, his children may not be getting enough food to eat.

> "Tobacco growing is a key element of the economy in many developing countries in Africa and South America."
>
> *The Tobacco Manufacturers' Association*

Tobacco also has an environmental cost. Many developing countries grow tobacco for export but do not grow enough food crops to feed their own people. Tobacco plants need lots of chemical fertilizers, which can make the land unfit for growing food.

Thousands of acres of forest are cut down to provide firewood to dry the tobacco leaves. One tree is cut down every two weeks for each person who smokes twenty cigarettes a day.

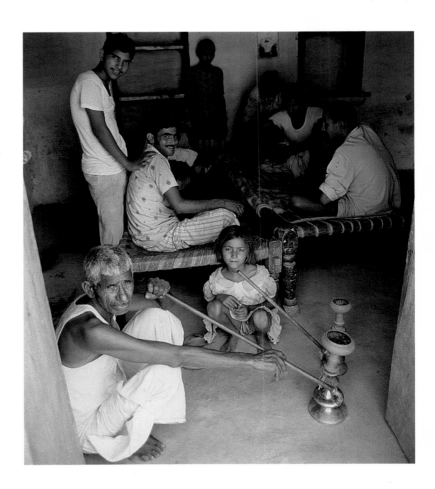

▶ *This man in India is smoking through a water pipe called a hookah.*

2. Becoming a smoker

Why do people start smoking?

Do any of your family or friends smoke? Do you know how old they were when they started smoking? People start smoking for different reasons. Most people who are regular smokers started smoking when they were in their early teens, or even younger.

Sometimes, people start smoking because they want to find out what it is like. Their first cigarette may make them feel sick or dizzy, but they see other people enjoying cigarettes, and they want to get the same feeling. After a while, they get used to smoking.

Many people think smoking looks cool, or grown-up. It first had this image in the 1930s. All the famous movie stars smoked, and their fans wanted to look like them. Films can make smoking look glamorous. Seeing movie or rock stars smoke makes some fans want to do so too, just as they want to dress or talk like them. Smoking is part of the image.

▲ Movie stars like Rita Hayworth made smoking look glamorous to our grandparents and great-grandparents.

"

"Every ... waking hour from billboards, TV screens, movies, radios, and now the Internet, the tobacco industry beckons our children."
World Health Organization Tobacco-Free Initiative

"

Some people start smoking to try to impress boyfriends or girlfriends or to fit in with a certain crowd. They are afraid they will be left out if they say they don't want to smoke. Friends can encourage people to smoke. If they are smokers, they want their friends to be like them, so they can smoke together and lend each other cigarettes. If your family or friends smoke, it can seem like the natural thing to do. Surveys show that children whose family or friends smoke are much more likely to become regular smokers themselves.

▲ *This young Rwandan boy lives on the streets. He has become a smoker and now has to beg for money for cigarettes as well as for food.*

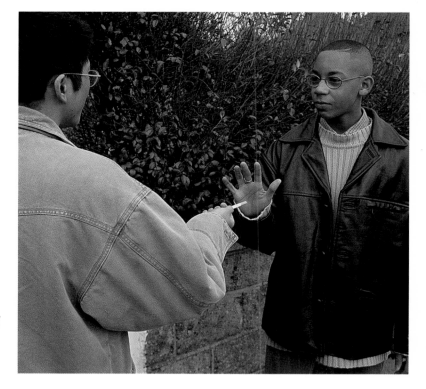

▶ *When friends offer cigarettes, it can be hard to refuse. But saying "no" shows that you know your own mind and aren't afraid to stand your ground.*

Smoking as a comfort

Sometimes, people start to smoke when they feel worried or are under stress. They might have changed schools or jobs or be taking important exams. They may have problems at home that no one seems to understand. Perhaps they feel they need something to help them get by, so they turn to cigarettes. Smoking can be comforting and help people to concentrate or to relax.

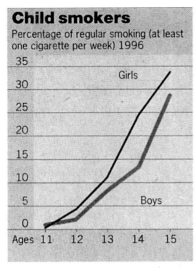

Child smokers
Percentage of regular smoking (at least one cigarette per week) 1996

Source: ONS Survey among secondary schoolchildren, quoted in The Guardian, *February 9, 2000*

▲ *This graph shows that one-third of 15-year-old girls in the United Kingdom smoked in 1996.*

▲ *Going to school can be stressful, especially if you have exams coming up.*

FACTS:
In the United States, 60% of smokers start smoking before they are 14 and 90% before they are 21. About 90% of teenagers who smoke a few cigarettes will become regular smokers. British surveys show that many people smoke their first cigarette between the ages of 9 and 12.
(Source: Health Education Authority, UK)

case study · case study · case study ·

Leanne started smoking when she was thirteen, after her grandmother Ellen died. Leanne and her grandmother had been really close. Leanne sometimes felt her grandmother was the only person who understood her. Ellen had been a heavy smoker. When she was sixty, she became ill with lung cancer. She was sick for about a year before she died. Everyone said she was her own worst enemy because she wouldn't give up smoking.

After her grandmother died, Leanne had a rough time at school. She didn't have any close friends and she missed her grandmother a lot. When she started smoking, it felt as if she were somehow getting closer to her. Everyone became angry with Leanne too, as they had been with Ellen. The first time Leanne's mother saw her smoking she was really shocked. She said, "You're going to end up just like your grandmother."

"I started smoking around the time I changed schools. It was hard to make new friends at first, and everything was strange. Then I got in with a new crowd. They all seemed to smoke, so I did too. It makes you feel like you belong."

Dan, age 14

▶ *Every day of every year, families lose loved ones to smoking-related diseases. Smoking is the biggest cause of lung cancer.*

A way of rebelling

Smoking can be a way of rebelling against teachers or parents. Most people now know that smoking can harm their health. But smoking can be like wearing a badge that says "I am old enough to decide for myself. If I want to smoke, I will. If I want to risk my health, I can, because it is my body."

Some people point out that the health warnings on cigarette packages may even encourage some people to smoke. Smokers like to feel they can take risks and are not scared by the warnings. Taking risks may even be a way of proving that they feel grown-up and in control. This is why one U.S. manufacturer made cigarettes with the brand name "Death."

"In the young smoker's mind, a cigarette falls into the same category as wine, beer, shaving, wearing a bra… a declaration of independence and striving for self-identity."
Extract from a marketing report for the tobacco industry

◀ *These children in Brazil are hanging out with teenagers, who can encourage them to start smoking early.*

"
"They are always warning us about something, aren't they? Don't eat this, don't do that. You risk your life every time you cross the road, don't you?"

Nina, aged 15

"

◀ *Young people may think it is cool to smoke.*

What does smoking say about you?

♦ This is my body, OK?
♦ I can take risks
♦ I am a bit of a daredevil
♦ I can handle this
or
♦ I don't mind if my breath and clothes smell of smoke
♦ I don't mind spending my money on tobacco
♦ I don't mind nicotine being in control of me
♦ I can cope with illness and disease

FACT:
In some Latin American cities, 50% of teenagers smoke. The younger people are when they first start to smoke, the higher their risk of getting lung cancer and other diseases. (Source: Health Education Authority)

3. "I need a cigarette"

Why is smoking addictive?

Have you ever heard a smoker say "I need a cigarette?" What do you think makes him or her feel this need? The smoker's body is telling him or her to smoke because it has become addicted to nicotine.

Nicotine can calm someone down when he or she feels worried or upset, or it can make a person feel lively and in control instead of tired or bored. It works quickly, so the smoker feels better almost immediately. The nicotine passes into tiny tubes in the lungs and then into the bloodstream. It reaches the brain in about seven seconds. Once a person has started smoking, his or her body gets used to nicotine and starts to need it. This is called addiction.

▲ A model of the human lungs. The tiny tubes shown here in pink and white are called bronchioles. They carry nicotine into a smoker's bloodstream.

FACT:
Nicotine is measured in milligrams per cigarette: the amount of nicotine ranges from less than 0.1 mg per cigarette to just over 1.0 mg. The drug is named after Jean Nicot, the courtier who started the fashion for smoking at the French royal court in the 16th century.

FACT:
Nicotine replacement products such as nicotine gum and skin patches can help smokers give up the habit. These products give low doses of nicotine without the other poisonous chemicals in tobacco smoke. They are safer and less addictive than cigarettes and help quitters get through the craving for nicotine.

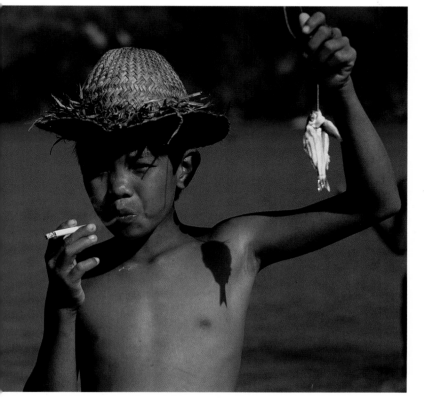

▲ This woman is using a nicotine inhaler. It gives a low dose of nicotine.

◀ This young boy in Indonesia feels proud that he is grown up enough to smoke.

17

Nicotine—as addictive as heroin

Soon after a cigarette has been smoked, the level of nicotine in a smoker's blood drops quickly. This can happen even faster if the person is eating, or feeling worried or nervous. The smoker starts to feel jumpy and can't relax. Soon, the person needs to smoke another cigarette to feel better again.

Nicotine is as addictive as heroin. As a smoker's body gets used to nicotine, the person needs to smoke more often. Smokers may start to feel the need to smoke every twenty to forty-five minutes to keep up the level of nicotine in their blood. Some people become chain-smokers, smoking up to sixty cigarettes a day.

"A cigarette is a carefully crafted product that delivers just the right amount of nicotine to keep its user addicted for life before killing the person."
Dr. Gro Harlem Brundtland, Director General of the World Health Organization

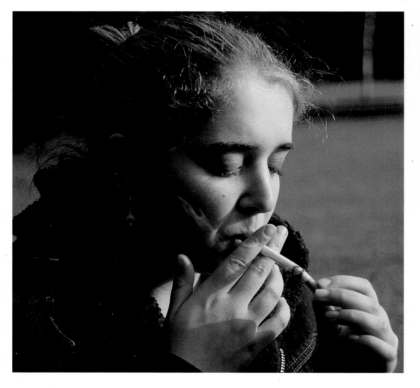

◀ *Some people chain-smoke—lighting one cigarette from another they are already smoking.*

It is easy to get hooked on cigarettes. People often start by smoking the occasional cigarette when they are out with friends. If they begin to smoke regularly, they may find they crave a cigarette when they are on their own too, and so they start to buy packs themselves. Once people are buying their own cigarettes, they are likely to smoke more.

"Smoking a cigarette for the beginner is a symbolic act. 'I am no longer my mother's child, I am tough, I am an adventurer...' But as the power of this idea fades away, the chemical effects of the drug take over, and the smoker gets hooked."
Adapted from a quote from the vice-president for Research and Development, cigarette manufacturer Philip Morris

◄ *Like many people, this young woman sits down to relax with a magazine and a cigarette.*

The smoking habit

Addiction means that the smoker's body starts to need nicotine, but also that he or she has started to rely on cigarettes to get through stressful times. Smoking quickly becomes a habit. Habits can be comforting and help us feel in control. Smokers get used to the feeling of a cigarette in their hand or mouth. They get used to carrying cigarettes and matches around with them. Cigarettes become part of their daily routine.

"Smoking is just part of being me. When I go out to teen clubs, I take my makeup, enough money for the club and a taxi, and my cigarettes. What else do you do while you are waiting for your friends to turn up?"

Shelley, aged 17

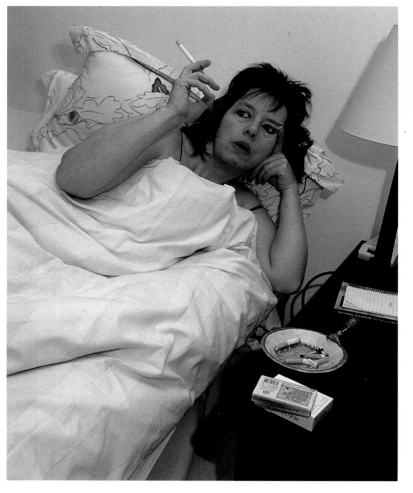

◀ *Research has shown that more than a third of smokers light up during the first fifteen minutes of their day.*

case study · case study · case study · case study · case study

Rajeema has smoked for years. She works in a local government office that has a no-smoking policy. When she is at work, Rajeema has to go and stand outside the building to have a cigarette. Some of her coworkers come out as well and they enjoy talking and smoking.

Rajeema also smokes when she is out with her friends. Smoking keeps her from feeling so shy when she meets someone new. People are always handing around cigarettes, and smoking makes Rajeema feel she is part of the crowd.

Rajeema's friend Jamila would like to give up because she wants to save money to get married next year, but it's hard saying no all the time. Sometimes, the guys make fun of Jamila because she doesn't want to smoke and won't drink because she is driving. Rajeema feels sorry for Jamila, but Jamila is determined to give up smoking.

▲ *Many smokers use coffee and lunch breaks to smoke. In cities, they can often be seen smoking outside offices that have no-smoking policies.*

Some people reach for a cigarette when they first wake up in the morning. Others smoke with a cup of coffee or after a meal. It is common for people to smoke when they are doing something stressful, such as working or driving. Cigarettes can also help people feel relaxed at parties, or when they meet new people for the first time.

4. The health risks of smoking

What are the risks of smoking?

How would you rate the health risks of smoking? Some people say that everything in life is a risk, and you have to die of something. But there are some risks you can avoid, such as smoking. It is something we can choose not to do, like running across a busy street.

There are more than 4,000 chemicals and gases in the smoke from a burning cigarette. Many of them are poisonous. When a smoker inhales, these chemicals pass into the body. They include:

♦ Carbon monoxide, a gas found in car exhaust fumes
♦ Nicotine
♦ Sticky black tar
♦ Traces of pesticides
♦ Poisonous metals such as arsenic and hydrogen cyanide, a poisonous liquid.

When a cigarette is smoked, smoke passes along the bronchial tubes leading to the lungs. These tubes are lined with tiny hairs that keep dirt and germs out of the lungs. Tobacco smoke damages the hairs so the bronchial tubes may become blocked and cannot keep out germs so well.

▲ *As this cigarette burns, thousands of poisonous chemicals are released. At least 40 are believed to cause cancer.*

Nicotine makes the heart beat faster and raises the blood pressure, putting extra strain on the smoker's heart. Carbon monoxide makes it harder for the blood to carry oxygen around the body. Carbon monoxide, along with nicotine, can thicken the blood, which can lead to heart disease.

Soot and tar stick to the lungs and the bronchial tubes. This can cause coughs and breathing problems and lead to lung diseases, including lung cancer, emphysema, and bronchitis.

▼ *A poster showing the dangers of tar. Light cigarettes have less tar and nicotine. But smokers may inhale them more deeply and take in the same amount of tar and nicotine as from normal cigarettes.*

FACTS:
Smoking causes 90% of deaths from lung cancer worldwide. Tobacco use is estimated to cause 20% of all deaths worldwide. Someone dies every 8 seconds from a smoking-related disease.
(Source: World Health Organization)

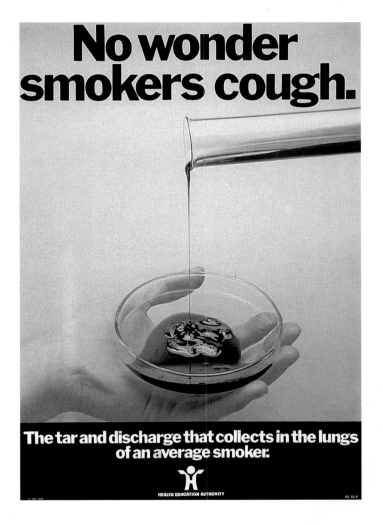

No wonder smokers cough.

The tar and discharge that collects in the lungs of an average smoker.

HEALTH EDUCATION AUTHORITY

Your health in the future

Smoking causes four times as many deaths as alcohol, drugs, traffic accidents, and all the other risks that we can try to avoid. But to many people, the risks of smoking do not seem real. When we are young, illnesses in later life may seem too far ahead to worry about. But many people who were not concerned when they were teenagers are today facing long illnesses. However old they are when they become ill, they will feel the same person inside as they did when they were young.

FACTS:
In the United States, about 400,000 people die each year from smoking-related diseases.
(Source: American Cancer Society)
Worldwide, 4 million people a year die from smoking-related diseases. By 2030, this figure is expected to rise to 10 million.
(Source: World Health Organization)

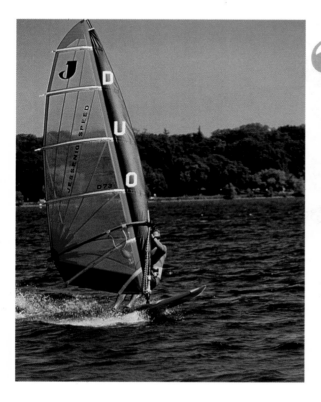

"Virtually every activity involves some potential risk, whether it be smoking, skiing, swimming or driving a car."
US tobacco company Philip Morris

◄ *Cigarette makers sometimes compare smoking with other risky but enjoyable pastimes such as windsurfing. Yet most sports improve rather than damage our health.*

case study · case study · case study · case study · case study

Every year for twenty years, Sheila made a New Year's resolution to give up smoking, but each time she failed. She was smoking two packs a day, and even when she lost her job as a store manager, and had little money, she kept smoking. If anything, she smoked more when she was out of a job. Often, money went on cigarettes rather than food.

Sheila and her husband felt things couldn't get much worse for them, but then Sheila found she had lung cancer. She had to have weeks of chemotherapy and radiotherapy. She lost her hair and felt tired and sick most of the time. Sheila's treatment can't cure her because the cancer has spread.

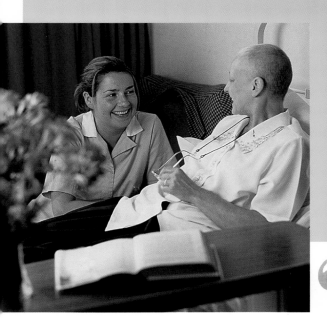

Sheila's two boys are in their teens. Some of their friends are already smokers. Sheila knows that they may start smoking because she took it up even though her own mother had died of cancer. Somehow, she felt it would never happen to her because she had always felt healthy until recently.

▲ *Cancer patients can face long illnesses. They may need to take strong anti-cancer drugs, which can cause side effects, such as making their hair fall out.*

"A cigarette is the only freely available consumer product, that, when regularly consumed as indicated, kills."
World Health Organization

The cost of the habit

If you smoke, your breath, hair, and clothes may all smell of stale tobacco smoke. Tar and nicotine make your teeth look yellow or gray, and tar can stain your fingers yellow. Tobacco smoke dries the skin and damages it. Even young smokers may show signs of aging as early as their twenties. Their skin may look dull and lines may form around the mouth and eyes. Smoking can also spoil the taste of food.

▼ *Smokers may age quickly. This young smoker already has wrinkles.*

Smokers are less fit than non-smokers. They often become breathless when they exercise. Few successful sports people or athletes are smokers. Many smokers have coughs because their bodies are trying to clear the lungs. They have more health problems than non-smokers. Someone who smokes twenty cigarettes a day is twice as likely to take time off work as a non-smoker.

◄ *We can tell that this man is a smoker by looking at his hands. His fingers and nails are badly stained by the tar from cigarettes.*

"I didn't think I smelled of smoke. I have always been really careful about cleaning my teeth properly and things like that. It really upset me when I kissed this girl and she told me my breath smelled like an ashtray!"

Josh, college student, age 19

FACT:
From 1950 to 2000, about 62 million people died from diseases caused by smoking. That is more than all the people killed in World War II.
(Source: World Health Organization)

▼ *Like many regular smokers, this girl suffers from a morning cough, as her lungs try to clear themselves.*

There is no "safe" level of smoking, and there is a health risk from all smoking, including herbal or low-tar cigarettes, cigars, and pipes. Half of all the people who become long-term smokers will be killed by tobacco.

Smokers also face the huge cost of their habit. It's estimated that someone who starts smoking at the age of twenty spends around $100,000—perhaps as much as buying their home—on cigarettes during his or her life.

"Cigarette smoking is now as important a cause of death as were the great epidemic diseases such as typhoid, cholera, and tuberculosis that affected previous generations in this country."
The British Royal College of Physicians

5. Living and working with smokers

What is passive smoking?

Do you think it is right to ban smoking from public places? Some smokers think that they should be able to smoke wherever they want. But now that we know more about the risks of passive smoking, many people believe that non-smokers have the right to clean air.

Passive smoking means breathing in someone else's cigarette smoke. When someone smokes a cigarette, they only inhale 15 percent of the smoke. The rest goes into the air. Being in a smoky room can make some people feel dizzy and give them coughs, red eyes, sore throats, headaches, and breathing problems. Scientists believe that passive smokers are 10 to 30 percent more likely to get lung cancer than people who do not live or work with smokers.

"After I have been to work, the next morning I am coughing like a smoker. I used to think it wasn't worth giving up cigarettes because working in a bar is just like smoking."

Nicole, bartender and waitress

▶ *These women in a bar in Paris are lighting up while they have a drink. In the United States, some bars have banned smoking, but smokers' rights groups have fought against the ban.*

► Cinemas used to be smoky places until no-smoking areas were introduced. Now, smoking is banned in most movie theaters in the United States.

"Even if smokers are a minority, their needs should still be met."
Tobacco Manufacturers' Association

In Europe and the United States, smoking is now banned in many public places such as buses, cinemas, and restaurants. Other places may have no-smoking sections. Many companies are adopting no-smoking policies. They are worried they might be taken to court for failing to protect their workers from passive smoking.

Denmark has the highest rate of smoking in the European Union and the highest rate of women smokers in the world. A law passed in 1996 banned smoking in all public buildings. Health projects were set up to help people quit.

FACTS:
In the United States, research has shown that around 3,800 people a year die from lung cancer caused by passive smoking.
(Source: U.S. Environmental Protection Agency)
A recent U.S. study found that people who work in bars and restaurants are one and a half times more likely to get lung cancer than the rest of the population.

Children's health

Almost half of all children worldwide—700 million children—live in the homes of smokers. Children who smoke, or live with smokers, are more likely to develop coughs, colds, and breathing problems. They have higher levels of carbon monoxide in their blood and get tired more easily. If they have asthma, smoking can make it worse.

When both parents smoke at home, a child may be subject to passive smoke as if they smoked 80 cigarettes a year. Even pet cats and dogs can have skin and breathing problems because they are passively smoking their owners' cigarettes.

▲ This baby in Java, Indonesia, has to breathe in his father's smoke. The child of a smoker is twice as likely to smoke as the child of a non-smoker.

◄ If a pet lives in the home of a smoker, it can suffer health problems from passive smoking.

case study · case study · case study · case study · case study

Carol started smoking when she was fourteen. She tried to give up when she became pregnant several years later. Although she cut down, she kept smoking. As her family grew, she tried not to smoke around her children, especially when they had colds or infections.

Carol had heard of asthma but she didn't know much about it until the doctor said that her ten-year-old daughter, Angela, and nine-year-old son, Lennie, were both asthmatic. Carol's doctor warned her that passive smoking would make the children's breathing problems worse. Carol tried not to smoke when the children were home from school, but she still enjoyed having a cigarette when she was watching television or after a meal. When Lennie was eleven, he had a really bad asthma attack and had to be rushed to the hospital. Carol knew she had to stop smoking completely, not just for her own health but for the sake of the children.

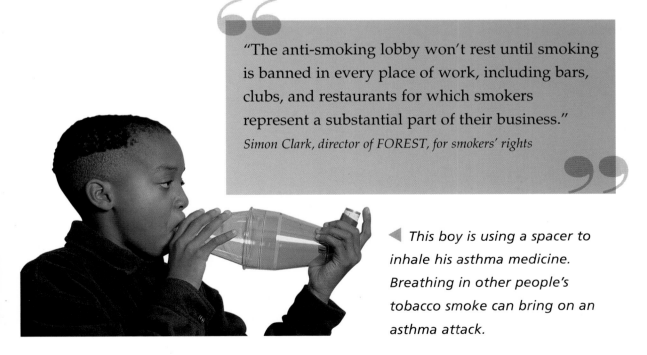

"The anti-smoking lobby won't rest until smoking is banned in every place of work, including bars, clubs, and restaurants for which smokers represent a substantial part of their business."
Simon Clark, director of FOREST, for smokers' rights

◀ *This boy is using a spacer to inhale his asthma medicine. Breathing in other people's tobacco smoke can bring on an asthma attack.*

Smoking in pregnancy

When a pregnant woman smokes, her baby becomes a passive smoker. The chemicals from cigarettes pass into the mother's bloodstream, and then to her baby. Nicotine makes the baby's heart beat faster. The carbon monoxide means that less oxygen gets to the baby. The baby does not grow as much as it should. Pregnant women who smoke have a higher risk of losing the baby in pregnancy or of having a premature, stillborn, or low-weight baby.

Women who smoke when they are pregnant may have problems with their own health. They are more likely to get ill and have to go into the hospital during their pregnancy. But it can be hard for a pregnant woman to quit. Some women are worried they will put on too much weight if they stop smoking. Others feel they need cigarettes to help them through the stresses of the pregnancy.

▲ When a woman is pregnant, it can be hard coping with everyday chores and worries. Some women turn to cigarettes, even though they know the health risks to themselves and their babies.

◄ A 20-week-old baby boy in the womb. He is almost fully formed—and he may already be the victim of passive smoking.

They might be worrying about money, housing or relationships, and what will happen once the baby is born.

About two-thirds of women who smoke give up during their pregnancy. Others manage to cut down the number of cigarettes they smoke. This can mean that they inhale more deeply when they do smoke, but that is not always the case. If a woman stops smoking before she becomes pregnant, or in the early months of pregnancy, she can reduce the health risks to herself and her baby.

FACT:
A smoker's baby weighs an average 200 grams less than a non-smoker's. Smaller babies are more likely to become sick or even die.

"I'd been a smoker for six years before I got pregnant. I'd tried giving up before, but once I knew about the baby, I stopped just like that. I think it was when they warned me about the risk of premature birth. I didn't want to take any risks with my baby."
Debbie, age 24

◄ *Women who choose not to smoke in pregnancy give their babies a head start to good health.*

33

6. The profits from tobacco

Why is smoking big business?

Why is growing tobacco so popular? Tobacco makes a lot of money for tobacco growers, manufacturers, store owners, and governments. Worldwide, the tobacco industry earns more than $275 billion a year in sales.

Tobacco is grown in about a hundred countries around the world. Often, farmers can make more money growing tobacco rather than food. In the United States, farmers receive about 40 times more income from an acre of tobacco than they do for an acre of wheat. In countries such as Venezuela, tobacco manufacturers provide a fixed price for tobacco growers and help them with farming technology.

> "Every time someone buys tobacco products, they are supporting an industry that goes for profit before people, without regard for human suffering or environmental cost."
>
> *GASP Smoke-free Solutions*

International tobacco companies are among the richest companies in the world. In the United States, the profits from tobacco are higher than the profits made by the giant computer firms.

▶ *These farmers are harvesting tobacco leaves on a farm in Cuba.*

But nowadays, fewer people in developed countries are buying cigarettes. For example, in the United States, tobacco sales are falling by about 2 percent a year. Also, some people are taking the tobacco companies to court because of diseases caused by smoking.

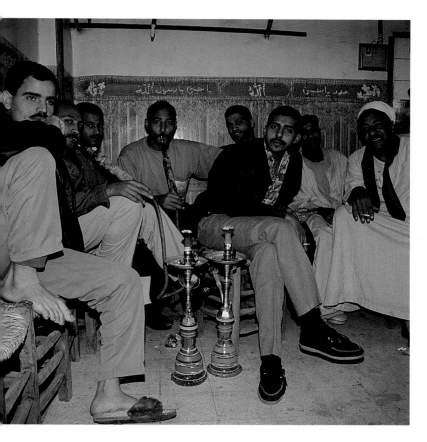

▲ These men in a café in Cairo, Egypt, are smoking a hookah together. The tobacco used in hookahs is often high in tar and nicotine.

The tobacco companies have started to put their money into other businesses, such as food and drinks. They are also selling more cigarettes in developing countries. For example, China now consumes around 30 percent of the world's cigarettes. Another 30 percent are smoked in the growing markets of South America, the Middle East, Africa, and Asia.

High-tar brands and cigarettes without filters have become less popular in richer countries because of health warnings. They are now being sold to developing countries.

The tobacco companies continue to make huge profits, but they make them from different parts of the world.

35

Cigarette advertising—making smoking look glamorous

How many cigarette brands can you name? Cigarette manufacturers spend millions of dollars every year to make people aware of their brands.

In the United States, tobacco companies spend an estimated $11 million every day advertising their products—more than the U.S. Federal Office on Smoking and Health spends in an entire year to discourage smoking. In some countries, tobacco companies sponsor sports and other events to make people aware of their brands. They also advertise by paying film-makers to show movie stars smoking their brand; this is called indirect advertising. The tobacco industry claims that it is not trying to encourage new smokers but to persuade people who already smoke to switch brands.

> "There is no convincing evidence that tobacco advertising causes anybody—adult or child—to start smoking."
> *Tobacco Manufacturers' Association*

► *The tobacco industry likes to link smoking with fast, glamorous sports. Sports, such as motor racing, have come to rely on sponsorship money from tobacco companies.*

13mg TAR 0·9mg NICOTINE
SMOKING WHEN PREGNANT HARMS YOUR BABY
Health Departments' Chief Medical Officers

MAIDEN

◀ *Advertisers think up clever ideas to make people aware of their brands. Sometimes, they do not even show the product.*

Some countries, including New Zealand, Canada, Norway, Sweden, and Finland, have banned all cigarette advertising. In Norway, research shows that since advertising was banned in 1975, people are smoking fewer cigarettes, and the number of children taking up smoking has halved.

In 1998, the European Union passed a law to ban all direct advertising in member states. The British tobacco industry is fighting government proposals to ban advertising and sponsorship by tobacco companies. It needs to find 330 new smokers a day to replace those who have died from diseases caused by smoking.

> "The tobacco companies…make you believe that if you smoke, you're going to be sexy, attractive, successful, accepted by your peers…they project this image in every media—from daytime soap operas to movies, magazines, and even cartoons."
>
> *Tobacco control activist Allen Landers*

The tobacco industry—who pays and who benefits?

Governments earn billions of dollars in taxes every year from the tobacco industry. In Denmark, 84 percent of the price of a pack of cigarettes is tax. The British Government received over $16 billion in tax from the tobacco industry in 1998. But every year, billions of dollars are spent on caring for smokers who have become ill. Millions of work days are lost, too. The World Bank estimates that the world economy loses at least $200 billion a year because of the use of tobacco products.

"The tobacco industry is a major contributor to the British economy…[in one year] it would, for example, pay for three-quarters of the Education and Employment budget or 40 Millennium Domes."

The Tobacco Manufacturers' Association

▲ *Many smokers will end up spending a large amount of time in hospitals. In the United States, medical care for tobacco-related diseases costs $50 billion each year.*

More companies are now becoming aware of the costs to their businesses and their workers of illnesses caused by smoking. Some have adopted rules against smoking and plans to encourage employees to quit smoking.

case study · case study · case study · case study · case study

Last year, Jamie was out sick from his factory for a total of thirty working days. Jamie is a heavy smoker. He has always had difficulty breathing, and even a cold or flu can leave him unwell with a nasty cough and breathing problems for several weeks. Recently, Jamie has begun to have pains in his chest and arms. Doctors have told him he has heart trouble, made worse by his smoking habit. Jamie's employers know that his sick record is getting worse every year. They have always allowed their staff to smoke but now they are considering a no-smoking policy at work. Every year they lose hundreds of working days because of illness among their staff. A report on smoking in the workplace found that smokers take almost a third more sick leave every year than non-smokers. This costs businesses billions of dollars per year.

◀ *Another day off work because of illness*

7. Quitting the habit

How can you stop smoking?

Do you know anyone who has given up smoking? Most smokers decide at some time that they would like to give up the habit. They may be worried about their health or need to stop spending so much money on cigarettes.

Smokers must really want to give up if they are going to succeed. Some fail because they don't want to give up enough or because they are only giving up to please someone else, like a partner or a doctor. Some may feel they cannot cope with life without their cigarettes. Others say they are giving up, but think it will be all right if they have a cigarette now and again.

▲ Nicotine patches deliver up to 1 mg of nicotine an hour. It passes through the skin into the bloodstream to stop the craving.

◀ Chewing gum can help smokers quit. Some people use nicotine gum that releases a low dose of nicotine.

The first days or weeks after giving up can be hard, because the smoker's body finds it difficult to do without nicotine. During this time, people may have headaches and feel nervous and jumpy. As the level of carbon monoxide in the blood falls, more oxygen gets to the brain, so the person may start to feel dizzy or find it hard to sleep. People feel cravings for a cigarette, especially when they are under stress or others around them are smoking.

These young people are at a group counseling session for ex-smokers. Only 1 to 3 percent of people manage to quit without any help.

Some smokers try using nicotine gum or patches on the skin to help them get through the first weeks. Others get help from counselors or join a no-smoking group, where everyone supports one another. Hypnosis and acupuncture can help some people quit.

FACTS:
In the United States, 70% of adult smokers say they want to quit. About 1.5 million of them quit smoking every year.
(Source: National Centers for Disease Control and Prevention)
About 54% of smokers in Great Britain say they want to quit. Around 1,000 people a day do stop smoking.
(Source: QUIT)

Quit Day

These hints can help people who want to quit:

♦ Cut down smoking gradually—or

♦ Stop on a particular day, such as New Year's Day or World No Tobacco Day, when lots of other smokers are trying to give up

♦ Keep a smoker's diary before the Quit Day. The smoker writes down when he or she is most likely to reach for a cigarette and thinks of other things to do instead, such as

♦ Chewing gum instead of smoking

♦ Taking up exercise

♦ Eating healthy foods, such as fruits, instead of smoking.

▲ Giving up smoking does not need to mean putting on weight. Eating a healthy diet and exercising will help an ex-smoker keep in shape.

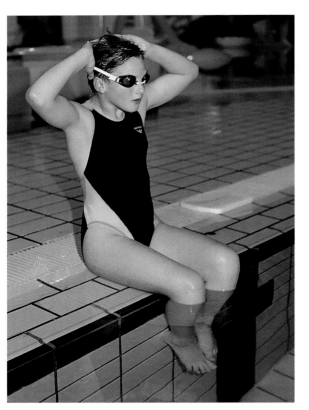

Some people worry that they will put on weight when they stop smoking because they will be tempted to eat more. Food certainly tastes better if you don't smoke, and ex-smokers may find that their weight increases slightly. It usually balances after a month or two.

◄ This girl is about to enjoy a swim. Being a non-smoker is part of living a healthy life.

John is in his early forties. He started smoking when he became a truck driver in his twenties, going through about $2^1/_2$ packs of cigarettes a day. Smoking and listening to the radio made the job a bit less boring. When he got home, John always felt too tired to exercise, until his partner Sandra bought a puppy. John found himself taking the growing dog for long walks at the weekends.

It was then that John began getting bad pains in his legs. He went to the doctor, who told him that his blood had become thick and sticky. The arteries in his legs were so clogged that there was a risk that John could lose his legs, or die. John knew that his only chance was to give up smoking and become more fit. It was hard because he had always had a pack of cigarettes in his cab. John got used to smoking a dummy cigarette and used nicotine skin patches to help him over the first few weeks. With Sandra's support he stopped smoking altogether. Now when he feels like having a cigarette, he takes the dog out instead.

▶ Getting out and about, but keeping away from places where people are likely to smoke, can make it easier to quit.

Feeling healthy again

Smokers who give up understand the health risks and what it means to be addicted to a drug like nicotine. They know that even if they feel bad when they first give up, they will soon start to feel better.

When smokers quit, they will begin to feel more fit and less breathless when they exercise. They will smell nicer, their clothes will no longer smell of stale tobacco smoke, and their skin will look better.

"If you want to stop smoking, any method can help. If you don't want to stop, no method will help."
The Health Education Authority

▼ *Non-smokers have more money to spend on things they enjoy; these boys saved up for their bikes.*

Ex-smokers find that their teeth and fingers gradually lose the tar stains. They feel better about themselves because they are no longer relying on a drug to get through life, and they have more money to spend on things that are good for them.

After a few weeks, the blood circulation improves and after a few months, the lungs start to clear and work properly. Gradually, the health risks are reduced. After about fifteen years, an ex-smoker has the same risk of early death as a non-smoker.

"I felt awful at first. I was told it was the body's reaction to getting rid of all that garbage. Now I feel so much better."
James, finalist in QUIT's awards for UK Quitter of the Year, 1999

◀ *These girls have been training for a running event. Choosing not to smoke is a lifestyle choice, like choosing a favorite sport or fitness activity.*

"You have to understand what's going on in your head…when I want a cigarette I think, "but wouldn't it be awful to go through all that again." For one cigarette it's just not worth it."
Lauren, ex-smoker

GLOSSARY

Acupuncture
A way of treating addiction, pain, or illness by pricking the skin with needles.

Addiction
A desperate need or dependence on something, such as a drug. Addicts cannot give up their habits without help.

Asthma
An illness that causes breathing problems.

Bronchial
To do with the lungs.

Bronchitis
A disease that inflames the air tubes in the lungs.

Chain-smoker
Someone who smokes continuously, often lighting up a cigarette from the one he or she is already smoking.

Chemotherapy
The treatment of disease, especially cancer, using chemical substances.

Craving
The strong need or desire for something.

Emphysema
A disease that damages and destroys lung tissue.

Epidemic disease
A disease that spreads very widely among people in an area at a certain time.

Filter
The part at the top of many cigarettes that removes some of the poisonous chemicals so that the smoker doesn't breathe them in.

Herbal cigarettes
Cigarettes made from a mixture of herbs instead of tobacco.

Hookah
A type of Turkish pipe that cools the smoke as it passes through a pot filled with water.

Hypnosis
Putting someone into a kind of sleep in order to treat them, for example, for addiction.

Inhale
To breathe in, for example, air or tobacco smoke.

Nicotine
A chemical in cigarettes that makes smokers keep wanting to smoke.

Passive smoking
Breathing in other people's cigarette smoke.

Pesticides
Chemicals used to kill insects harmful to crops.

Premature
Too early; before the normal time.

Radiotherapy
The treatment of cancer and other diseases using X rays.

Snuff
Powdered tobacco that is sniffed through the nose.

Sponsor
To give money for a sports or arts event as a way of advertising a product.

Stillborn
When a baby is born dead.

Tar
A thick, sticky substance in tobacco that collects in the lungs. Different cigarettes have different amounts of tar (high-tar, low-tar, etc.)

ORGANIZATIONS

United States
ASH (Action on Smoking
and Health)
2013 H Street NW
Washington, DC 20006
http://ash.org

Americans for Nonsmoker's
Rights
2530 San Pablo Ave
Suite J, Berkeley
California 94702

Office on Smoking and Health
at Centers for Disease Control
Mail Stop K-50
4770 Buford Highway NE
Atlanta
Georgia 30341-3742

UK
ASH (Action on Smoking
and Health)
102 Clifton Street
London EC2A 4HW
Tel: 020 7739 5902
www.ash.org.uk
Campaigns for policies to
control the health problems
caused by tobacco

GASP Smoke-free Solutions
93 Cromwell Road
Bristol BS6 5EX
Tel/fax: 0117 942 5185
Resources on tobacco control
and smoking education

QUIT
Victory House
170 Tottenham Court Road
London W1P 0HA
Tel: 020 7388 5775
Smokers Quitline 0800 002200
Helps smokers quit

WDM (World Development
Movement)
25 Beehive Place
London SW9 7QR
Tel: 0201 7737 6215
www.wdm.org.uk
Campaigns against tobacco use
and promotion in the
developing world

WEBSITES
www.tobacco.org
A wealth of information on
everything to do with tobacco

www.infact.org
Information on the tobacco
industry

FURTHER READING

De Angelis, Gina. *Nicotine and Cigarettes* (Junior Drug Awareness). Chelsea House, 1999.

Gosselin, Kim. *Smoking Stinks* (Substance Free Kids). JayJo Books, 1998.

Haughton, Emma. A Right to Smoke? (Viewpoints). Franklin Watts, 1997.

Royston, Angela. Learn to Say No: Smoking. Heinemann, 2000.

INDEX